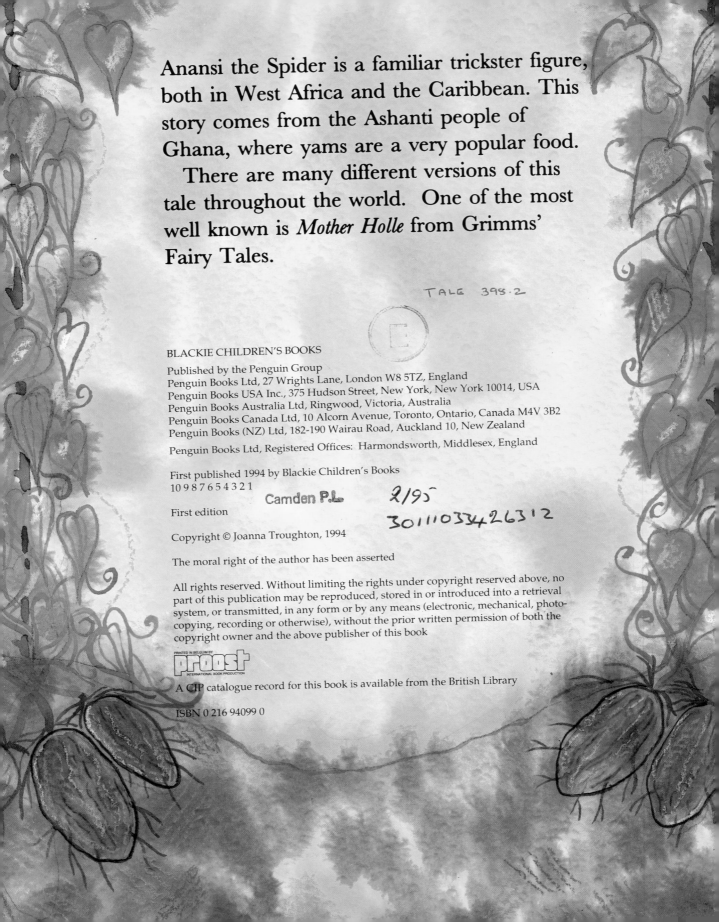

Anansi the Spider is a familiar trickster figure, both in West Africa and the Caribbean. This story comes from the Ashanti people of Ghana, where yams are a very popular food.

There are many different versions of this tale throughout the world. One of the most well known is *Mother Holle* from Grimms' Fairy Tales.

TALE 398.2

BLACKIE CHILDREN'S BOOKS

Published by the Penguin Group
Penguin Books Ltd, 27 Wrights Lane, London W8 5TZ, England
Penguin Books USA Inc., 375 Hudson Street, New York, New York 10014, USA
Penguin Books Australia Ltd, Ringwood, Victoria, Australia
Penguin Books Canada Ltd, 10 Alcorn Avenue, Toronto, Ontario, Canada M4V 3B2
Penguin Books (NZ) Ltd, 182-190 Wairau Road, Auckland 10, New Zealand

Penguin Books Ltd, Registered Offices: Harmondsworth, Middlesex, England

First published 1994 by Blackie Children's Books
10 9 8 7 6 5 4 3 2 1

Camden P.L   2/95

First edition   3011103342 6312

Copyright © Joanna Troughton, 1994

The moral right of the author has been asserted

PRINTED IN BELGIUM BY
proost
INTERNATIONAL BOOK PRODUCTION

A CIP catalogue record for this book is available from the British Library

ISBN 0 216 94099 0

FOLK TALES OF THE WORLD

A WEST AFRICAN FOLK TALE

ANANSI and the MAGIC YAMS

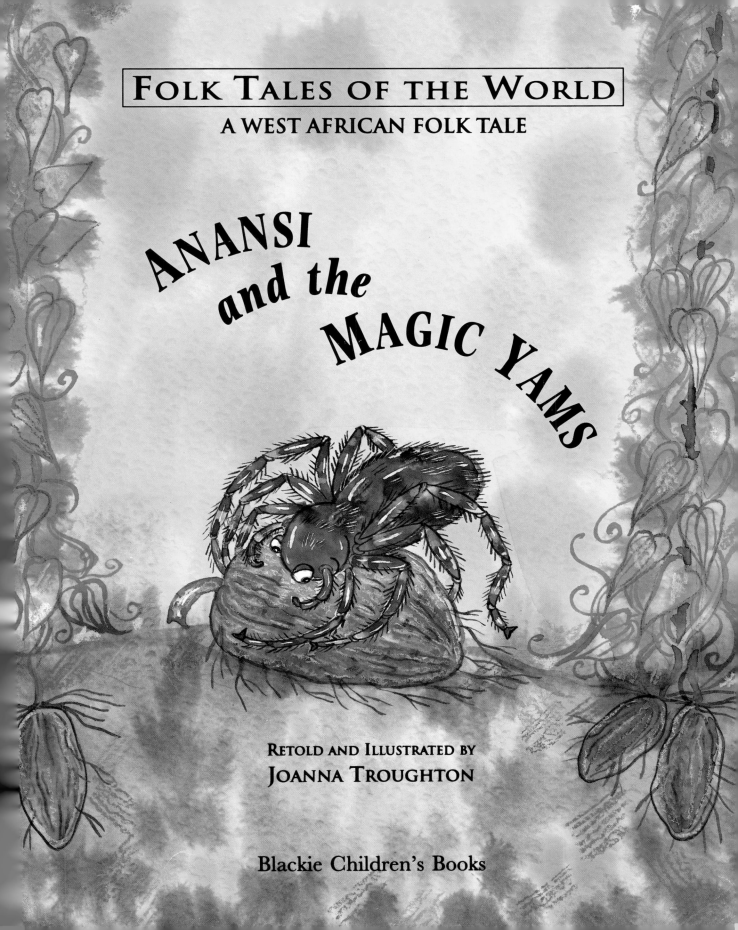

RETOLD AND ILLUSTRATED BY
JOANNA TROUGHTON

Blackie Children's Books

One year the yams didn't grow
and the animals were all hungry.

Anansi's son went into the forest to search for food. He found one palm nut, but it rolled away down a hole in the ground.

Anansi's son followed the palm
nut. He let himself down the hole
on a creeper. At the bottom of the
hole was a beautiful garden.

The garden was tended by three Spirits. The three Spirits were very dirty. They looked as if they hadn't washed themselves or cut their hair since the beginning of time. But Anansi's son was too polite to say so.

'Why have you come to our garden?' asked the Spirits.

'I followed a palm nut,' said Anansi's son. 'Our yams didn't grow this year and all the animals are hungry.'

'Go and dig some yams from our garden,' said the Spirits kindly. 'But don't pick the biggest ones which will say, "Take me, take me."'

Anansi's son went to dig up some yams. The biggest yams said, 'Take me, take me.' But Anansi's son only took the smaller ones.

Then the Spirits said, 'When you return home, peel the yams, throw away the insides and cook the peels.'

There were two baskets in the garden. One was big and one was small.

'Which basket would you like for your yams?' asked the Spirits.

Anansi's son was not greedy.

'I'll take the small one, please,' he said.

Then the Spirits taught him a song:

'Red Spirit ho! ho!
Blue Spirit ho! ho!
White Spirit ho! ho!
Should my head disobey
What would befall me?'

'Sing this song secretly when the
basket is empty, and it will fill up with
yams again.'

Anansi's son thanked the Spirits.
He took his basket and climbed
back out of the hole.

Anansi's son peeled the yams, threw away the insides and cooked the peels. He gave them to the hungry animals. They were delicious. When the basket was empty, he sang the song secretly to himself, and the basket filled up with yams again.

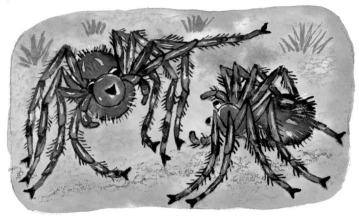

Anansi saw that his son was a hero.

'Please show me the hole in the ground,' he begged.

'Tomorrow,' said Anansi's son.

Anansi couldn't sleep. He was so excited. Before the sun was up he was rattling the water jars.

'It is morning,' he lied. 'Lion is carrying water from the well.'

'Go to sleep,' said his son.

Anansi swept the floor.

'It is morning,' he lied. 'Hyena is sweeping the yard.'

　'Go to sleep,' said his son.

Anansi took a bundle of twigs and set them alight.

'It is morning,' he lied. 'See, the sun is rising.'

　'Go to sleep,' said his son.

Finally the sun came up. Anansi's son led Anansi into the forest and showed him the hole in the ground.

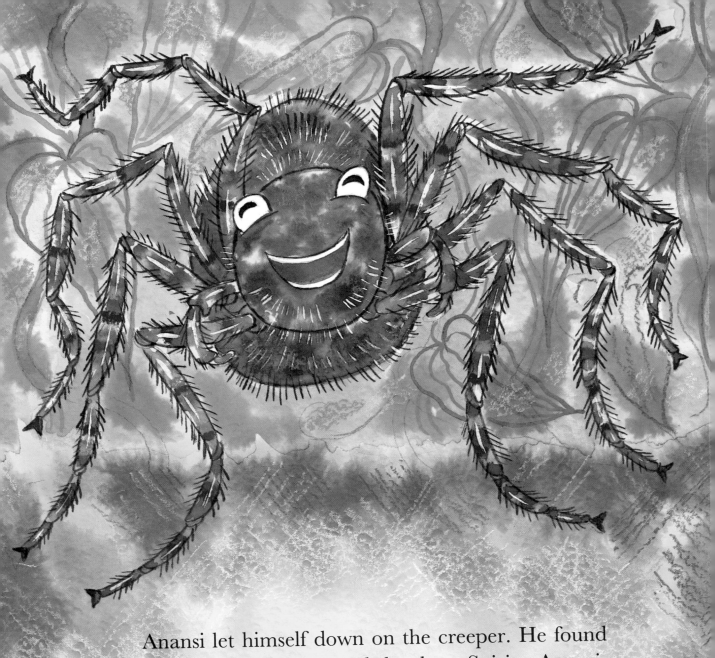

Anansi let himself down on the creeper. He found
the beautiful garden and the three Spirits. Anansi
was not polite like his son. He did not keep his
thoughts to himself.

'Pooh!' he exclaimed. 'You three haven't washed
yourselves or cut your hair since the beginning of
time.' And he laughed rudely.

But the three Spirits spoke kindly to Anansi.
   'Go and dig some yams in our garden,' they said.
'But don't pick the biggest ones which will say,
"Take me, take me."'
   Anansi was greedy. He took no notice of the
Spirits' words. He picked the biggest yams which
said, 'Take me, take me.'

The Spirits said, 'When you return home, peel the yams, throw away the insides and cook the peels.'

'Only a fool would do that,' Anansi said.

'Which basket would you like?' asked the Spirits.

Of course Anansi chose the big one.

Then the Spirits taught Anansi the magic song, and
told him to sing it secretly when he wanted more
yams.

Anansi climbed out of the hole, dragging his
basket behind him. He didn't even say thank you.

'Gather round,' said Anansi.
'See, I have a bigger basket than my son's.'
Anansi peeled the yams, threw away the peels and cooked the insides. But he didn't give his yams away. Instead he sold them for gold and cowrie shells.

And when the animals ate the yams they
found them as hard as stones.
The basket was empty, so Anansi sang the
song loudly for everyone to hear:

'Red Spirit ho! ho!
Blue Spirit ho! ho!
White Spirit ho! ho!
Should my head disobey
What would befall me?'

But the basket was still empty and
the animals began pointing at
Anansi. He looked down at himself
and saw that he was covered in
horrible spots and boils.

Anansi crept away into the forest.
He stayed there until he was healed.
But you can still see the traces of
spots and boils on a spider's back
today. It is a reminder of how rude
and greedy Anansi the Spider was
when he picked the magic yams.